Curious George DiSCOVERS the Seasons

Adaptation by Cynthia Platt

Based on the TV series teleplay written by Joe Fallon

Houghton Mifflin Harcourt

Boston   New York

Photographs on the cover and pages 7 (top), 11, 14 (bottom), 20, 26 (bottom), 30, and 31 (middle and bottom) courtesy of HMH/Carrie Garcia

Photographs on pages 9, 12, 14 (top), 31 (top), and 32 courtesy of HMH

Photograph on page 7 (bottom) courtesy of Kevin Sawford

Photographs on page 25 courtesy of Trevor Morris

Photograph on page 26 (top) courtesy of Steve Allen

Art adaptation by Rudy Obrero and Kaci Obrero

ISBN: 978-0-544-78586-1 paper over board

ISBN: 978-0-544-78509-0 paperback

www.hmhco.com

Printed in China

SCP 10 9 8 7 6 5 4 3 2 1

4500599931

George was a good little monkey and always very curious. Do you want to hear about the time George's curiosity helped him learn all about the seasons?

It all started on a cold winter day. The leaves were gone and the grass was brown, but there wasn't a snowflake in sight. George had to bundle up in his winter coat. But when he got outside, he wasn't sure what to do.

There were no fallen leaves to play in. There were no birds to watch.
George had toys for warm days and toys for snowy days, but nothing
for just plain cold days.

George had an idea. He would visit with the bunnies! But when he went next door, the bunnies weren't in their hutch. He found his friend Bill and the bunnies inside. "I'm going to bring them to my grandmother's house for the winter, George," Bill told him. "It's just too cold here to keep the bunnies outside in their house."

George was disappointed to see the bunnies go. Then Bill asked him to do a special job. "While I'm away, will you feed Jumpy Squirrel for me?" he asked. "There aren't a lot of nuts and seeds around in winter, so it's an important job."
George was happy to help!

Did you know . . .

animals deal with the change of seasons in completely different ways than we do? Some animals hibernate. That means they stay in one place for the winter. They become less active to save their energy for spring. Their heart rates and breathing slow down and their body temperature drops like when they're sleeping. Other animals migrate, or move to warmer parts of the world when winter comes.

George fed Jumpy, but that took only a minute.

He wasn't sure what to do after that.

He looked around his yard and thought about summer.

He missed his pool and blowing bubbles.

Everything fun seemed to happen in the spring, summer, or fall. Winter was the most boring season.

George decided he wasn't going to let winter ruin his fun. It might not actually be summer, but he could still do summertime things.

George got the hose and filled his little pool with water. But when he jumped in, the water was so cold! George got cold, too. Brrr . . .

He ran into the house. "Soak your feet in warm water to get rid of the chill," the man with the yellow hat said. The warm bath was a lot nicer than the cold pool. George felt much better.

The next day it was even colder! George bundled into his coat and scarf when he went out to play. He wanted to enjoy being outside in the winter as much as he would in the other seasons. He sat by his pool to relax.

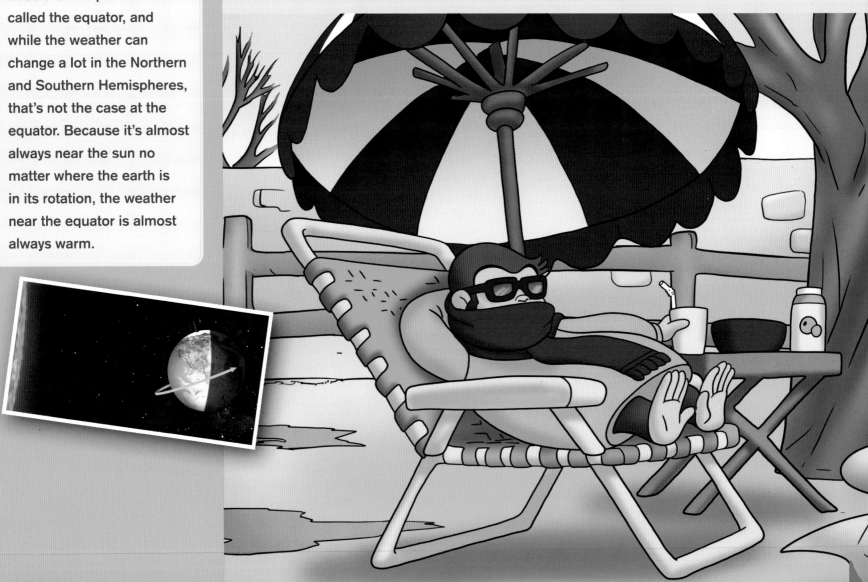

Then George blew some bubbles for Jumpy. But when Jumpy tried to pop a bubble, they discovered that it had frozen. George didn't know bubbles could freeze.

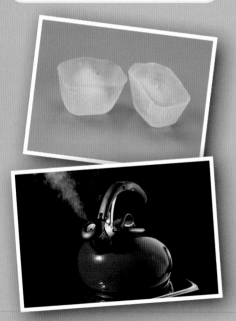
That was a surprise! Then George noticed something even more surprising: the water in the pool had frozen. Yesterday's summer fun had turned into today's giant ice cube!

George was starting to feel like an ice cube too. He went inside to warm up and drink some hot cocoa.

George was puzzled. How could a monkey have any fun outside when everything kept freezing?

Suddenly, George had an idea! He could use frozen things to
make a game. He filled a balloon and several cartons
from the recycling bin with water.

Then he brought them outside so they would freeze in the cold air.

George didn't notice when Jumpy accidentally spilled some seeds and nuts into the cartons of water.

The next morning was the coldest day yet! George had to wear a hat, scarf, and coat to stay warm. He didn't mind, though. He went to check on the balloon and cartons of water he'd left out the night before. They were frozen solid! George couldn't wait to set them up for a game of icy winter bowling.

Test it out!

You can freeze objects in water too. All you need is a freezer-safe plastic container and a variety of objects. Fill the container with water and then add berries or small pieces of fruit. Place the full container in the freezer for a couple of hours and then remove your giant ice cube. Be sure to take note if the fruits you put in sank to the bottom or stayed near the top of the ice. Are the ones that sank heavier or lighter than the ones that floated near the top?

When he took the ice from the cartons, though, he realized that some of Jumpy's nuts and seeds were frozen inside. Oh, well. George decided to try to bowl anyway.

But Jumpy kept trying to break his breakfast out of the ice! George had an idea. He broke the ice into pieces so Jumpy could find the nuts.

The pieces slid on the ground and Jumpy chased after them. George and Jumpy knocked the ice blocks around until the sun went down. It wasn't ice bowling, but it was just as fun!

Besides, George knew he could try his new bowling invention again the next day. He filled the cartons and balloon with water once more and left them outside.

In the morning, George bundled up. "You're not going to need that hat and scarf today, George," his friend said. George went outside. It felt more like spring or fall than winter. George checked on his cartons and balloon, hoping for another round of ice bowling. But the water hadn't turned to ice — it was too warm for it to freeze!

The weather was very confusing. Wasn't it supposed to be cold in the winter and warmer in the other seasons? George went back into the house.

But later that day, something amazing happened! George thought he saw something outside his window. When he went to look, it was snowing.

George thought that if it was cold enough to snow, it might be cold enough for water to freeze again. And cold enough to make a new ice bowling set. Maybe the cold could be fun after all!

George realized that winter, spring, summer, and fall were all great in their own way. But the pool could wait until summer.

Right now, he had winter toys to play with —
and a whole chilly season to enjoy!

Exploring the Seasons: Winter, Spring, Summer, Fall

George had a case of the winter blues, but then he discovered that no matter what the season, there are lots of great things to do. While you can only jump in colorful leaves in the fall and watch new things sprout and grow in spring, you can watch the weather any time of year and keep track of what you learn about each season's traits by starting your very own weather journal.

You will need . . .

- a notebook
- markers, crayons, or colored pencils
- your five senses

What to do:

First, write down the date so you know which day and season it is when you look back through your journal. Then write down a few words about what the weather looks like that day. Is it sunny, rainy, cloudy, windy? Does the temperature feel cold or warm—or dry or humid? What can you smell when you take a deep breath?

Once you write down your description, it's time to illustrate! Use your crayons, markers, or colored pencils to draw a picture of what the day looks like, being sure to capture as many details and colors of the season that you can. You can write in your weather journal every day, or even once a week or once a month, to help keep track of how the seasons change near you!

Frozen Fun

Test it out!

No matter what the season, you can create your own icy bowling set.

You will need . . .

- 3 to 5 milk cartons, washed out and open at the top
- medium-size balloons
- a freezer (or a cold winter night)

What to do:

Fill your clean cartons almost to the top fold with water. Fill the balloon with water and ask an adult to firmly tie the top closed so that no water leaks out. Leave the cartons and balloon in the freezer or outside overnight. Then slip the ice blocks out of the cartons and peel the balloon away from the frozen globe of ice. (If you made the ice in the freezer, be sure to bring it outside before taking it out of the containers.) Set up the blocks in a triangle and roll the ball of ice to knock down the blocks. Play alone or with friends until the ice melts!

Who's Hungry? You Are!

Here's a frosty — and healthy — treat you can make and enjoy whenever you need a snack.

You will need . . .

- your favorite fruit juice
- ice pop molds (or an ice cube tray with waxed paper and craft sticks)

What to do:

Ask a parent or friend to help you fill an ice pop mold. If you don't have one, fill the segments of the ice cube tray with juice and then cover with waxed paper. Stick one toothpick or craft stick through the waxed paper into each segment of juice. This will help keep the sticks in place as the juice freezes. Put the mold or ice cube tray in the freezer for about four hours until frozen solid. Enjoy a frosty treat.

Explore Further

Do different liquids freeze at different temperatures? You can find out — and track your results!

You will need . . .

- small paper cups
- water and other liquids (juice, oil, milk, soda)
- a cookie sheet
- a clock or timer
- paper and pen

What to do:

Place the paper cups on the cookie sheet, then fill each cup halfway with a different liquid. Carefully place the sheet in the freezer. Set your timer for one half hour. While you wait, make a chart of the liquids you used and leave a space to fill in how long it takes for each to freeze. Check on the cups when the timer goes off. Is anything frozen yet? Check again in another half an hour and another. Keep track of how long it takes for each type of liquid to freeze!